D0552142

THIS BOOK BELONGS TO:

Other Kipper books

Kipper
Kipper's Toybox
Kipper's Birthday
Kipper's Snowy Day
Where, Oh Where, is Kipper's Bear?
Kipper's Book of Colours
Kipper's Book of Opposites
Kipper's Book of Counting
Kipper's Book of Weather
Kipper's Christmas Eve
Kipper's A to Z
Kipper's Monster
Little Kipper Story Collection
Kipper Story Collection

Hisss!

Mick Inkpen

Hodder
Children's
Books

A division of Hachette Children's Books

The sun was making
a shadow of Kipper
on the wall.
It was a hot day.
A very hot day.

Kipper lay on his blanket, and sucked his drink through a curly-wurly straw.

'Today is a paddling pool kind of day,' he said.

The paddling pool
was on the top shelf
of the toy cupboard.

Kipper grabbed it and
pulled enthusiastically.

The toys in the cupboard
fell on Kipper's head.

Ouch!

It was hard work blowing up the paddling pool.

So when Kipper was finished, he turned on the hose and went to buy an ice cream.

On the way back the ice cream melted down Kipper's paw, and plopped into a puddle.

'That's odd,' said Kipper. 'It wasn't raining when I left.'

The puddle was as big as a pond. In the middle was Kipper's paddling pool looking very saggy.

'I know what has happened,' said Kipper.

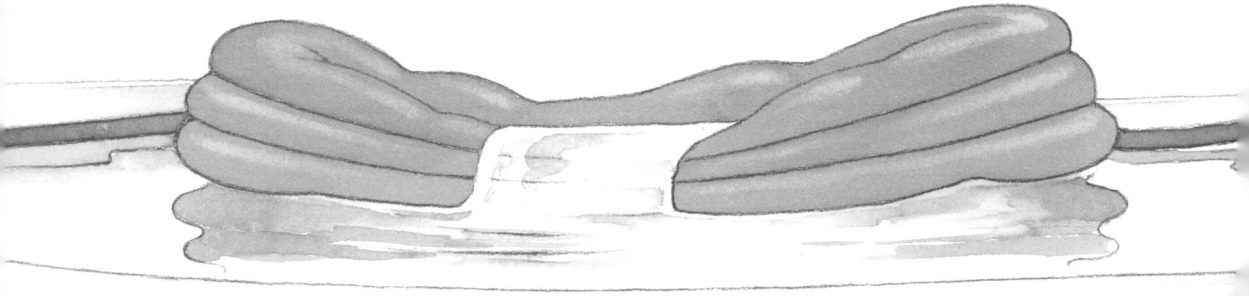

Kipper knelt down and listened very carefully to the paddling pool.

With his big ears he could just hear a tiny,

tiny

hisssssss

ssssss!

Kipper took the sticking plaster from his head.

Ouch!

And he mended the paddling pool . . .

. . . which was clever,
wasn't it?

First published 1999
by Hodder Children's Books,
a division of Hachette Children's Books,
338 Euston Road, London NW1 3BH

Copyright © Mick Inkpen 1999

10 9 8 7 6 5 4 3 2 1

ISBN: 978 0 340 736913

This edition published 2007 for Index Books Ltd

A catalogue record for this book
is available from the British Library.
The right of Mick Inkpen to be identitfied
as the author of this work
has been asserted by him.

All rights reserved

Printed in Hong Kong